Mr. McMouse

Mr. McMouse

by Leo Lionni

Alfred A. Knopf 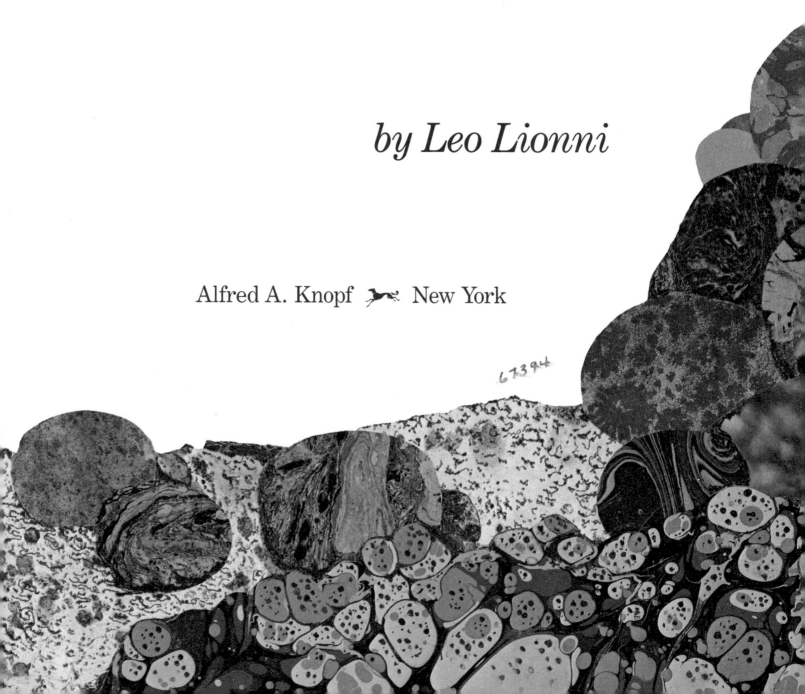 New York

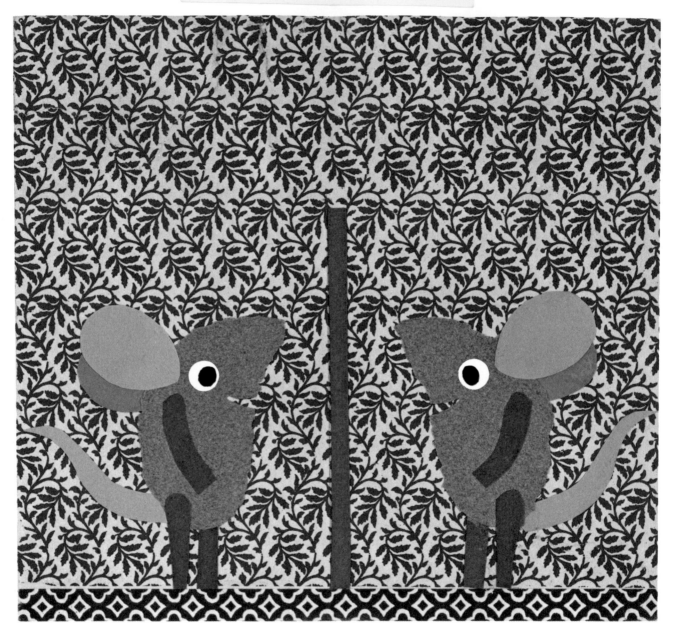

Whenever Timothy saw himself in the mirror, he felt happy.
"What a good-looking city mouse I am!" he thought.

But one day, instead of himself, Timothy saw a strange creature
dressed in black staring at him from the mirror.
He jumped back, let out a shriek, and ran for his life.

Timothy ran out of the building that had been his home
from the day he was born. And he kept running,
all the way to the outskirts of town.

Only when he came to the country road
did Timothy dare to slow down and think things over.
What had happened? Where could he go?
He knew that he couldn't go back home —
no one would recognize him in his new guise.
He had no choice. He had to go on.
But first he needed a quiet place to rest.

It was not long before he found a charming spot
where tall weeds grew among colorful rounded pebbles.
As he was catching his breath, he heard a noise.
Some field mice were observing him from behind the large boulders.
They looked frightened.

Timothy was frightened too.
How could he possibly explain
that he was nothing but an ordinary,
innocent city mouse?

Suddenly the weeds parted,
and a little field mouse stepped boldly forward.
"Hello," she said, "I'm Spinny. What's your name?"
"I am . . . I am . . . ," mumbled Timothy, confused.
The field mice stared at him.
Spinny smiled. "Never mind," she said.
"I'll give you a name: Mister McMouse!"
Timothy was surprised.
"How did you know I was a mouse?"
"Who else but a mouse
would have a tail like yours?"
said Spinny.

Then, as the other mice went about their business,
Spinny pointed to a beautiful mound of boulders.
"We live over there in the castle. Come with me.
Perhaps you can stay with us," she said.
Timothy, who felt that he had found a friend,
was happy to follow her.

As they went, Spinny explained all the things
he should know and do if he chose to live in the castle.
"If you want to stay for good," she warned,
"you will have to get a field mouse license,
and for that you'll have to pass some tests.
But don't worry.
I'll arrange everything."

The very next day the tests began,
and the first one was the Tickleberry Test.
"You see, field mice don't eat cheese," Spinny told Timothy.
"Only nuts, berries, and grain. But that will be easy.
Tickleberries are delicious."

When the mice had assembled on the test grounds,
Spinny led Timothy to the berry heap.
She then climbed high into the lookout tree to watch the show.
But alas, the test did not last long.
After a few berries, Timothy gave up.
"I'm sorry," he said. "I just can't eat berries.
They make me sick."

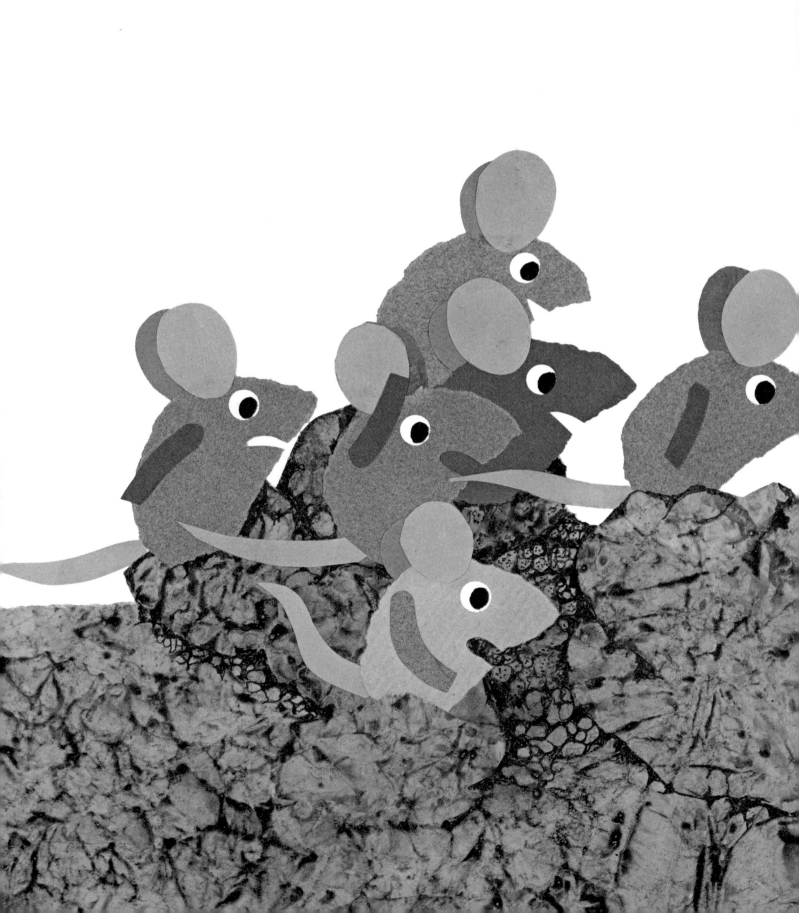

Next, Timothy was supposed to run to the heather field and back.
But he got only as far as the field,
where Bonyback, the turtle, found him lying in the heather,
hopelessly out of breath.

"Here is Mr. McMouse," said Bonyback. "He was lucky to find a cab."
Everyone laughed, except Timothy.
He knew that without a license he would have to leave.

Now there was one more test left, the Tree Climbing Test.
"Cheer up, Mr. McMouse," said Spinny.
"I am sure you can pass this one!"

Timothy got off to a good start.
But when he was halfway up the trunk,
Spinny saw a black cat slowly nearing the tree,
its muscles taut, ready for a leap.
"C-A-A-A-T!" she yelled as loud as she could.

In less than a second, all the mice had disappeared.
Only Timothy and Spinny were still running,
                    the cat a few feet behind.

Just as the cat was about to pounce on them,
Timothy saw an old rusty trap lying half-hidden in the weeds.
"Inside!" he shouted, pulling Spinny with him.
The cat slid to a sudden halt.
"What now?" said Spinny in a desperate little voice.
"You'll see," said Timothy, pulling Spinny
as close to the back wall as he could.

The cat hesitated, yawned, and lay down right in front of the trap.
Timothy smiled mysteriously. "Don't worry," he whispered.
Then he looked the cat straight in the eye, and
with the softest voice he could muster, he sang this lullaby:

Close your eyes and call your sheep.
Count them as they run and leap.
One, two, three, four, five, six, seven,
All these sheep will go to heaven.
Go to sleep. It's getting late.
Dreams will bring you number eight.

By now the cat was peacefully snoring away.
"This is our moment, Spinny," Timothy whispered.

They tiptoed out of the trap, and off they ran.

On License Day groups of chatty mice
gathered in Castle Square.
When finally the Headmouse called
Spinny and Timothy to the speaker's stand,
there was thundering applause,
for by now every mouse in the castle knew their story.
And when the Headmouse handed Timothy
an Honorary Field Mouse License
and Spinny a special medal for bravery,
happier mice had never been seen.

Leo Lionni was born in Holland and taught himself to draw by copying the work of the old masters in Amsterdam's museums. He received a Ph.D. in economics from the University of Genoa, in Italy, and came to this country in 1939 with his wife, Nora, and their two young sons. He has been involved in the world of graphic arts ever since. Internationally recognized as an artist, designer, sculptor, and author of children's books, he is the recipient of the 1984 American Institute of Graphic Arts Gold Medal and is a four-time Caldecott Honor Book winner for *Inch by Inch, Swimmy, Frederick*, and *Alexander and the Wind-Up Mouse.*

The Lionnis divide their time between a New York City apartment and a seventeenth-century farmhouse in the Tuscan hills of Italy.

THIS IS A BORZOI BOOK PUBLISHED BY ALFRED A. KNOPF, INC.

Copyright © 1992 by Leo Lionni
All rights reserved under International and Pan-American Copyright Conventions. Published in the United States by Alfred A. Knopf, Inc., New York, and simultaneously in Canada by Random House of Canada Limited, Toronto. Distributed by Random House, Inc., New York. Manufactured in the United States of America   10 9 8 7 6 5 4 3 2 1

Library of Congress Cataloging-in-Publication Data

Lionni, Leo, 1910–
Mr. McMouse / by Leo Lionni.
p.   cm.
Summary: Timothy, a city mouse who has been transformed into a tiny man, searches for his true identity among a group of field mice.
ISBN 0-679-83890-2 (trade). — ISBN 0-679-93890-7 (lib. bdg.)
[1. Mice—Fiction. 2. Identity—Fiction.] I. Title. PZ7.L6634Mr 1992
[E]—dc20 92-8963